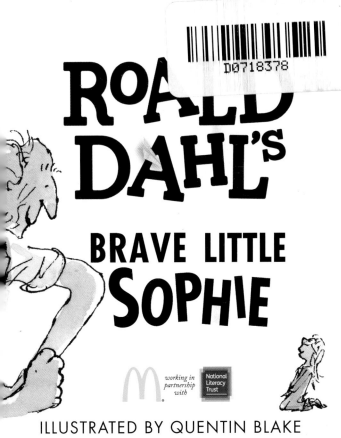

# ROALD DAHL'S

# BRAVE LITTLE SOPHIE

working in partnership with National Literacy Trust

ILLUSTRATED BY QUENTIN BLAKE

PUFFIN

PUFFIN BOOKS

UK | USA | Canada | Ireland | Australia
India | New Zealand | South Africa

Puffin Books is part of the Penguin Random House group of companies
whose addresses can be found at global.penguinrandomhouse.com.

www.penguin.co.uk    www.puffin.co.uk    www.ladybird.co.uk

Penguin
Random House
UK

Made for McDonald's 2017
001

*The BFG:* first published by Jonathan Cape 1982
Published in paperback by Puffin Books

Printed in Slovakia

A CIP catalogue record for this book is available from the British Library

ISBN: 978–0–141–38636–2

Batch nr: 128354/16

Meet

# BRAVE LITTLE
# SOPHIE!

A **LONELY** little girl from
an orphanage is about to
meet someone absolutely
**EXTRAORDINARY!**
Read on to find
out who . . .

Turn to the
back of your book
for **STICKERS**
and a handy
**BOOKMARK**

## SEARCH and FIND!

Sophie can't see without her **GLASSES**.
Can you **COUNT HOW MANY TIMES** they appear
in this book, starting from the next page?
Don't forget to check your stickers and bookmark!

## THE WITCHING HOUR

Sophie couldn't sleep.

A brilliant moonbeam was slanting through a gap in the curtains. It was shining right on to her pillow.

The other children in the dormitory had been asleep for hours.

Sophie closed her eyes and lay quite still. She tried very hard to doze off.

It was no good. The moonbeam was like a silver blade slicing through the room on to her face.

The house was absolutely silent. No voices came up from downstairs. There were no footsteps on the floor above either.

The window behind the curtain was wide open, but nobody was walking on the pavement outside. No cars went by on the street. Not the tiniest sound could be heard anywhere. Sophie had never known such a silence.

Perhaps, she told herself, this was what they called the witching hour.

The witching hour, somebody had once whispered to her, was a special moment in the middle of the night when every child and every grown-up was in a deep deep sleep, and all the dark things came out from hiding and had the world to themselves.

The moonbeam was brighter than ever on Sophie's pillow. She decided to get out of bed and close the gap in the curtains.

You got punished if you were caught out of bed after lights-out. Even if you said you had to go to the lavatory, that was not accepted as an excuse and they punished you just the same. But there was no one about now, Sophie was sure of that.

She reached out for her glasses that lay on the chair beside her bed. They had steel rims and very thick lenses, and she could hardly see a thing without them. She put them on, then she slipped out of bed and tip-toed over to the window.

When she reached the curtains, Sophie hesitated. She longed to duck underneath them and lean out of the window to see what the world looked like now that the witching hour was at hand.

She listened again. Everywhere it was deathly still.

The longing to look out became so strong she couldn't resist it. Quickly, she ducked under the curtains and leaned out of the window.

In the silvery moonlight, the village street she knew so well seemed completely different. The houses looked bent and crooked, like houses in a fairy tale. Everything was pale and ghostly and milky-white.

Across the road, she could see Mrs Rance's shop, where you bought buttons and wool and bits of elastic. It didn't look real. There was something dim and misty about that too.

Sophie allowed her eye to travel further and further down the street.

Suddenly she froze. *There was something coming up the street on the opposite side.*

*It was something black . . .*

*Something tall and black . . .*

*Something very tall and very black and very thin.*

It wasn't a human. It couldn't be. It was four times as tall as the tallest human. It was so tall its head was higher than the upstairs windows of the houses. Sophie opened her mouth to scream, but no sound came out. Her throat, like her whole body, was frozen with fright.

This was the witching hour all right.

The tall black figure was coming her way. It was keeping very close to the houses across the street, hiding in the shadowy places where there was no moonlight.

On and on it came, nearer and nearer. But it was moving in spurts. It would stop, then it would move on, then it would stop again.

But what on earth was it doing?

Ah-ha! Sophie could see now what it was up to. It was stopping in front

of each house. It would stop and peer into the upstairs window of each house in the street. It actually had to bend down to peer into the upstairs windows. That's how tall it was.

It would stop and peer in. Then it would slide on to the next house and stop again, and peer in, and so on all along the street.

It was much closer now and Sophie could see it more clearly.

Looking at it carefully, she decided it *had* to be some kind of PERSON.

Obviously it was not a human.
But it was definitely a PERSON.

A GIANT PERSON, perhaps.

Sophie stared hard across
the misty moonlit street. The
Giant (if that was what he
was) was wearing a long
BLACK CLOAK.

In one hand he was
holding what looked like a
VERY LONG, THIN TRUMPET.

In the other hand, he
held a LARGE SUITCASE.

13

The Giant had stopped now right in front of Mr and Mrs Goochey's house. The Goocheys had a green-grocer's shop in the middle of the High Street, and the family lived above the shop. The two Goochey children slept in the upstairs front room, Sophie knew that.

The Giant was peering through the window into the room where Michael and Jane Goochey were sleeping. From across the street, Sophie watched and held her breath.

She saw the Giant step back a pace

and put the suitcase down on the
pavement. He bent over and opened
the suitcase. He took something out
of it. It looked like a glass jar, one of
those square ones with a screw top.
He unscrewed the top of the jar and
poured what was in it into the end of
the long trumpet thing.

Sophie watched, trembling.

She saw the Giant straighten up
again and she saw him
poke the trumpet in
through the open

upstairs window of the room where the Goochey children were sleeping. She saw the Giant take a deep breath and *whoof*, he blew through the trumpet.

No noise came out, but it was obvious to Sophie that whatever had been in the jar had now been blown through the trumpet into the Goochey children's bedroom.

What could it be?

As the Giant withdrew the trumpet from the window and bent down to pick up the suitcase he happened to turn his head and glance across the street.

In the moonlight, Sophie caught a glimpse of an enormous long pale wrinkly face with the most enormous ears. The nose was as sharp as a knife, and above the nose there were two bright flashing eyes, and the eyes were staring straight at Sophie. There was a fierce and devilish look about them.

Sophie gave a yelp and pulled back from the window. She flew  across the dormitory and jumped into her bed and hid under the blanket.

And there she crouched, still as a mouse, and tingling all over.

18

After a minute or so, she lifted a corner of the blanket and peeped out.

For the second time that night her blood froze to ice and she wanted to scream, but no sound came out. There at the window, with the curtains pushed aside, was the enormous long pale wrinkly face of the Giant Person, staring in. The flashing black eyes were fixed on Sophie's bed.

# AN UNEXPECTED VISITOR

It's the witching hour and something is lurking outside Sophie's window. Can you join the dots to find out what it is?

# KIDNAPPED!

A huge hand with pale fingers came
snaking in through the window. This
was followed by an arm, an arm as
thick as a tree-trunk, and the arm,
the hand, the fingers were
reaching out across
the room
towards
Sophie's bed.

  This time
Sophie really did scream, but only
for a second because very quickly

the huge hand clamped down over her blanket and the scream was smothered by the bedclothes.

Sophie, crouching underneath the blanket, felt strong fingers grasping hold of her, and then she was lifted up from her bed, blanket and all, and whisked out of the window.

If you can think of anything more terrifying than that happening to you in the middle of the night, then let's hear about it.

The awful thing was that Sophie knew

exactly what was going on although she couldn't see it happening. She knew that a Monster (or Giant) with an enormous long pale wrinkly face and dangerous eyes had plucked her from her bed in the middle of the witching hour and was now carrying her out through the window smothered in a blanket.

What actually happened next was this. When the Giant had got Sophie

Colour me in!

23

outside, he arranged the blanket
so that he could grasp all the four
corners of it at once in one of his
huge hands, with Sophie imprisoned
inside. In the other hand he seized the
suitcase and the long trumpet thing
and off he ran.

Sophie, by squirming
around inside the blanket,
managed to push the top
of her head
out through
a little gap

just below the Giant's hand. She stared around her.

She saw the village houses rushing by on both sides. The Giant was sprinting down the High Street.

He was running so fast his black cloak was streaming out behind him like the wings of a bird.

Each stride he took was as long as a tennis court. Out of the village he ran, and soon they were racing across the moonlit fields. The hedges dividing the fields were no problem to the Giant.

25

He simply strode over them. A wide river appeared in his path. He crossed it in one flying stride.

Sophie crouched in the blanket, peering out. She was being bumped against the Giant's leg like a sack of potatoes. Over the fields and hedges

and rivers they went, and after a
while a frightening thought came into
Sophie's head. *The Giant is running fast,*
she told herself, *because he is hungry and
he wants to get home as quickly as possible,
and then he'll have me for breakfast.*

The Giant ran on and on. But now
a curious change took place in his way
of running. He seemed suddenly to
go into a higher gear. Faster and faster
he went and soon he was travelling
at such a speed that the landscape
became blurred. The wind stung
Sophie's cheeks. It made her eyes
water. It whipped her head back and
whistled in her ears. She could no
longer feel the Giant's feet touching
the ground. She had a weird sensation
they were flying. It was impossible to

tell whether they were over land or sea.
This Giant had some sort of magic
in his legs. The wind rushing against
Sophie's face became so strong that
she had to duck down again into the
blanket to prevent her head from
being blown
away.

Was it really
possible that
they were
crossing oceans?
It certainly felt that

way to Sophie. She crouched in the blanket and listened to the howling of the wind. It went on for what seemed like hours.

Then all at once the wind stopped its howling. The pace began to slow down.

Sophie could feel the Giant's feet
pounding once again over the earth.
She poked her head up out of the
blanket to have a look. They were in
a country of thick forests and rushing
rivers. The Giant had definitely slowed
down and was now running more
normally, although normal was a silly
word to use to describe a galloping
giant. He leaped over a dozen rivers.
He went rattling through a great forest,
then down into a valley and up over
a range of hills as bare as concrete,

and soon he was galloping
over a desolate wasteland that
was not quite of this earth.
The ground was flat and pale
yellow. Great lumps of blue rock were
scattered around, and dead trees stood
everywhere like skeletons. The moon
had long since disappeared and now
the dawn was breaking.

Sophie, still peering out from the
blanket, saw suddenly ahead of
her a great craggy mountain. The
mountain was dark blue and all

around it the sky was gushing and glistening with light. Bits of pale gold were flying among delicate frosty-white flakes of cloud, and over to one side the rim of the morning sun was coming up red as blood.

# JOURNEY TO GIANT COUNTRY

Can you work out which route the Giant must take to find his way home to Giant Country?

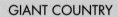

GIANT COUNTRY

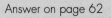
Answer on page 62

# THE CAVE

Right beneath the mountain, the Giant
stopped. He was puffing mightily.
His great chest was heaving in and out.
He paused to catch his breath.

Directly in front of them, lying
against the side of the mountain,
Sophie could see a massive round
stone. It was as big as a house.
The Giant reached
out and rolled the
stone to one side
as easily as if it

had been a football, and now, where the stone had been, there appeared a vast black hole. The hole was so large the Giant didn't even have to duck his head as he went in. He strode into the black hole still carrying Sophie in one hand, the trumpet and the suitcase in the other.

As soon as he was inside, he stopped and turned and rolled the great stone back into place so that the entrance to his secret cave was completely hidden from outside.

Now that the entrance had been sealed up, there was not a glint of light inside the cave. All was black.

Sophie felt herself being lowered to the ground. Then the Giant let go of the blanket completely. His footsteps moved away. Sophie sat there in the dark, shivering with fear.

*He is getting ready to eat me*, she told herself. *He will probably eat me raw, just as I am.*

*Or perhaps he will boil me first. Or he will have me fried. He will drop me like a*

*rasher of bacon into some gigantic frying-
pan sizzling with fat.*

A blaze of light suddenly lit up the
whole place. Sophie blinked and stared.
She saw an enormous cavern
with a high rocky roof.
The walls on either
side were lined with
shelves, and on the
shelves there
stood row
upon row of
glass jars.

There were jars everywhere. They were
piled up in the corners. They filled
every nook and cranny of the cave.

In the middle of the floor there
was a table twelve feet high and a
chair to match.

The Giant took off his black cloak
and hung it against the wall. Sophie
saw that under the cloak he was
wearing a sort of collarless shirt and
a dirty old leather waistcoat that
didn't seem to have any buttons. His
trousers were faded green and were

far too short in the legs. On his bare feet he was wearing a pair of ridiculous sandals that for some reason had holes cut along each side, with a large hole at the end where his toes stuck out. Sophie, crouching on the floor of the cave in her nightie, gazed back at him through thick steel-

41

rimmed glasses. She was trembling like a leaf in the wind, and a finger of ice was running up and down the length of her spine.

'Ha!' shouted the Giant, walking forward and rubbing his hands together. 'What has us got here?' His booming voice rolled around the walls of the cave like a burst of thunder.

# THE GIANT'S CAVE

Based on the descriptions you've read,
can you draw a picture of the
Giant's cave below?

# THE BFG

The Giant picked up the trembling
Sophie with one hand and carried her
across the cave and put her on the table.

*Now he really is going to eat me,*
Sophie thought.

The Giant sat down and stared hard
at Sophie. He had truly enormous ears.

Each one was as big as the wheel of a truck and he seemed to be able to move them inwards and outwards from his head as he wished.

'I is hungry!' the Giant boomed. He grinned, showing massive square teeth. The teeth were very white and very square and they sat in his mouth like huge slices of white bread.

'P . . . please don't eat me,' Sophie stammered.

The Giant let out a bellow of laughter. 'Just because I is a giant, you

think I is a man-gobbling cannybull!'
he shouted. 'You is about right! Giants
is all cannybully and murderful! And
they *does* gobble up human beans!
We is in Giant Country now! Giants
is everywhere around! Out there
us has the famous Bonecrunching
Giant! Bonecrunching Giant crunches
up two whoppsy-whiffling human
beans for supper every night! Noise is
earbursting! Noise of crunching bones
goes crackety-crack for miles around!'

'Owch!' Sophie said.

'Bonecrunching Giant only gobbles human beans from Turkey,' the Giant said. 'Every night Bonecruncher is galloping off to Turkey to gobble Turks.'

Sophie's sense of patriotism was suddenly so bruised by this remark that she became quite angry. 'Why Turks?' she blurted out. 'What's wrong with the English?'

'Bonecrunching Giant says Turks

is tasting oh ever so much juicier
and more scrumdiddlyumptious!
Bonecruncher says Turkish human
beans has a glamourly flavour. He says
Turks from Turkey is tasting of turkey.'

'I suppose they would,' Sophie said.

'Of course they would!' the Giant
shouted. 'Every human bean is
diddly and different. Some is
scrumdiddlyumptious and
some is uckyslush.'

Sophie was wondering
with a bit of a tremble what

all this talking about eating people was leading up to. Whatever happened, she simply must play along with this peculiar giant and smile at his jokes.

But were they jokes? Perhaps the great brute was just working up an appetite by talking about food.

'As I am saying,' the Giant went on, 'all human beans is having different flavours. Human beans from Panama is tasting very strong of hats.'

'Why hats?' Sophie said.

'You is not very clever,' the Giant

said, moving his great ears in and out.
'I thought all human beans is full of
brains, but your head is emptier than
a bundongle.'

'Do you like vegetables?' Sophie
asked, hoping to steer the conversation
towards a slightly less dangerous kind
of food.

'You is trying to change the subject,'
the Giant said sternly. 'We is having
an interesting babblement about the
taste of the human bean. The human
bean is not a vegetable.'

'Oh, but the bean *is* a vegetable,' Sophie said.

'Not the *human* bean,' the Giant said. 'The human bean has two legs and a vegetable has no legs at all.'

Sophie didn't argue any more. The last thing she wanted to do was to make the Giant cross.

'The human bean,' the Giant went on, 'is coming in dillions of different flavours. For instance, human beans from Wales

is tasting very whooshey of fish. There is something very fishy about Wales.'

'You mean whales,' Sophie said. 'Wales is something quite different.'

'Wales is *whales*,' the Giant said. 'Don't gobblefunk around with words. I will now give you another example.

Human beans from Jersey has a most disgustable woolly tickle on the tongue,' the Giant said. 'Human beans from Jersey is tasting of cardigans.'

'You mean jerseys,' Sophie said.

'You are once again gobblefunking!' the Giant shouted. 'Don't do it! This is a serious and snitching subject. May I continue?'

'Please do,' Sophie said.

'Danes from Denmark is tasting ever so much of dogs,' the Giant went on.

'Of course,' Sophie said. 'They

taste of great danes.'

'Wrong!' cried the Giant, slapping his thigh. 'Danes from Denmark is tasting doggy because they is tasting of *labradors*!'

'Then what do the people of Labrador taste of?' Sophie asked.

'Danes,' the Giant cried, triumphantly. 'Great danes!'

'Aren't you getting a bit mixed up?' Sophie said.

'I is a very mixed-up Giant,' the Giant said. 'But I does do my best.

And I is not nearly as mixed up as the other giants. I know one who gallops all the way to Wellington for his supper.'

'Wellington?' Sophie said. 'Where is Wellington?'

'Your head is full of squashed flies,' the Giant said. 'Wellington is in New Zealand. The human beans in

Wellington has an especially
scrumdiddlyumptious taste, so says the
Welly-eating Giant.'

'What do the people of Wellington
taste of?' Sophie asked.

'Boots,' the Giant said.

'Of course,' Sophie said. 'I should
have known.'

Sophie decided that this
conversation had now
gone on long enough.
If she was going
to be eaten, she'd

rather get it over and done with right
away than be kept hanging around any
more. 'What sort of human beings do
*you* eat?' she asked, trembling.

'*Me!*' shouted the Giant, his mighty
voice making the glass jars rattle on
their shelves. 'Me gobbling up human
beans! This I never! The others, yes!
All the others is gobbling them up
every night, but not me! I is a freaky
Giant! I is a nice and jumbly Giant! I
is the only nice and jumbly Giant in
Giant Country! I is THE BIG FRIENDLY

GIANT! I is the BFG. What is *your* name?'

'My name is Sophie,' Sophie said, hardly daring to believe the good news she had just heard.

Find out more about **BRAVE LITTLE SOPHIE** by visiting **ROALDDAHL.COM**

# WORD SCRAMBLE

The BFG often gets his words mixed up.
Can you work out what he is saying by
unscrambling the phrases below?

## 1. IGB YFINDELR IGATN
(Hint: p.57–58)

BIG FREINPLY Giant

## 2. GAITN OCNTUYR
(Hint: p.35)

GIANt CUntry

## 3. HAUNM EBASN
(Hint: p.46)

hymam be as

Answers on page 62

Use your stickers to decorate the journey to Giant Country!

# ANSWERS

## P.1: SEARCH AND FIND

Sophie's glasses appear 20 times in this book.

(On the following pages: 2, 5, 7, 19, 20, 32, 39, 42, 44, 47, 56, 58,
4 times on your sticker sheets and 4 times on your bookmark.)

## PP.34–35: JOURNEY TO GIANT COUNTRY

## P.59: WORD SCRAMBLE

1. BIG FRIENDLY GIANT

2. GIANT COUNTRY

3. HUMAN BEANS

## BOOKMARK

ROALD DAHL